# Horror [illegible] the [illegible]



by Roger Hu[illegible] West

Illustrated by Anthony Williams

**Titles in Alien Detective Agency 2**

| | |
|---|---|
| Pirate Planet | Roger Hurn/Jane A C West |
| Spiders from the Stars | Roger Hurn/Jane A C West |
| Horror in the Chamber | Roger Hurn/Jane A C West |
| The Day of the Scoffalot | Roger Hurn/Jane A C West |
| Slime Time | Roger Hurn/Jane A C West |
| Take Two | Jane A C West/Roger Hurn |
| Jack and Wanda Ride Again | Jane A C West/Roger Hurn |
| The Dark Side of the Moon | Jane A C West/Roger Hurn |
| Fan Club | Jane A C West/Roger Hurn |
| The Onyxx Star | Jane A C West/Roger Hurn |

Badger Publishing Limited
Oldmedow Road, Hardwick Industrial Estate,
King's Lynn PE30 4JJ
Telephone: 01438 791037
www.badgerlearning.co.uk

4 6 8 10 9 7 5 3

Horror in the Chamber ISBN 978-1-84926-942-1

First edition © 2012
This second edition © 2014



Publisher: Susan Ross
Senior Editor: Danny Pearson
Design: Julia King
Illustration: Anthony Williams

# Horror in the Chamber

## Contents

**Vocabulary:**

waxworks – a museum showing lifelike models of famous people made of wax

deerstalker – a soft cap with a bill at the front and back and ear flaps tied at the top

**Main characters:**

Jack Swift – the star of a top TV show

Wanda Darkstar – the Galactic Union's Alien Welfare Officer for Earth

Ima Smartie – a time-shifting alien criminal mastermind

Madam Grimm – the owner of Madam Grimm's Waxworks Museum

Sheerluck Holmes – a famous detective

Dr Whatsup – Sheerluck Holmes' assistant

## Chapter 1

# Ima Smartie

Jack had just finished a busy day filming the latest episode of 'Sci-Fi Spy Guy'. Now he was looking forward to going home and chilling out.

Jack chilled out by watching re-runs of his old shows on TV. He was his own biggest fan. Then he saw Wanda waiting outside the studio.

She did not look happy. "What's up, Wanda Woman?" he asked.

Jack had a feeling that he wasn't going to like the answer.

"Ima Smartie," said Wanda.

Jack frowned. "Maybe," he said, "but I'm even smarter!"

Wanda gave him a look that could burn a hole in concrete. It just bounced off Jack. "Ima Smartie is a time-shifting alien criminal genius," she said. "We have to catch her, but she is also a master of disguise, so nobody is sure what she really looks like."

"That's helpful," muttered Jack.

"Isn't it," said Wanda. "But Ima is wanted by every police force in the Galactic Union."

Jack shrugged. “So let them catch her,” he said. “I’m going home to watch TV.”

Wanda grabbed his arm and marched him back into the studio. “Oh no, you’re not,” she said. “This is a job for the Alien Detective Agency and, the last time I looked, you were still my crime-fighting partner.”

Jack groaned. “OK, so where is Ima Smartie hiding out? The Moon? Mars? Neptune?”

“None of those,” said Wanda as they climbed into STEALTH. “She’s right here in London.”

Jack rubbed his hands together with glee. “Great! That means we can nab her and I’ll still be home in time to watch ‘Sci-Fi Spy Guy versus the Lost Neck Monster’. It’s my all-time favourite episode.”

Wanda shook her head. “Sorry Jack, that isn’t going to happen. Remember I told you that Ima Smartie can time shift? She is in London – but London in the year 1889! We’re going to have to go back in time to catch her.”

## Chapter 2

# 221½ Baker Street

Jack and Wanda climbed out of STEALTH and found themselves in a large room.

Jack scratched his head. “Where are we, Wanda? And why has STEALTH landed in somebody’s house?”

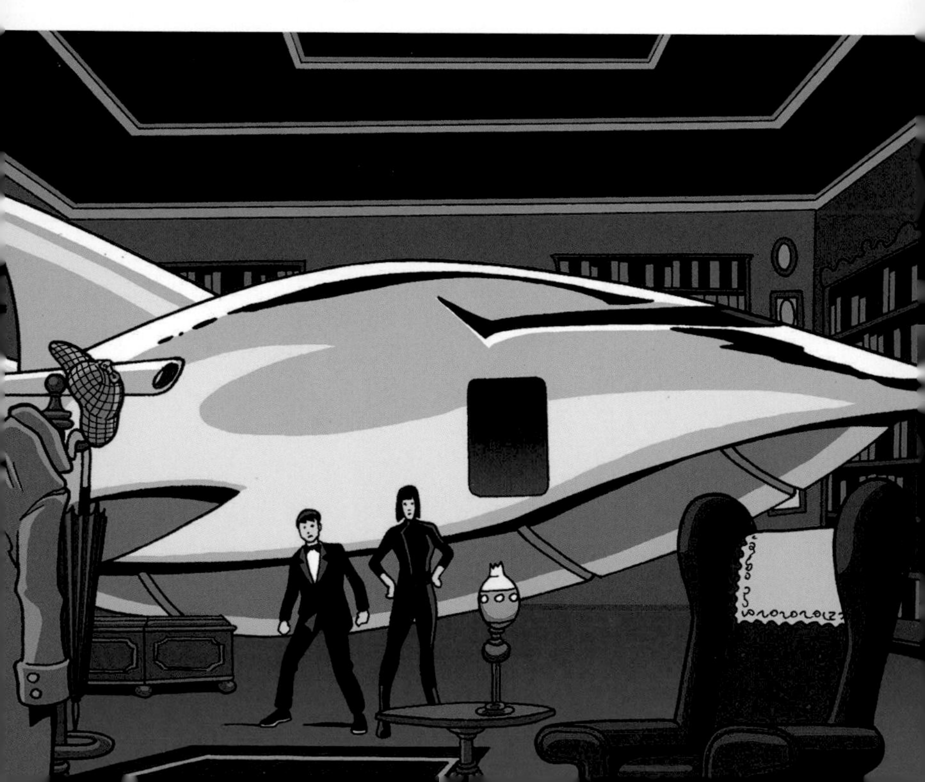

"We are in 221½ Baker Street, London – and this isn't just anybody's house. This is the home of the great Victorian detective, Sheerluck Holmes, and his friend Dr Whatsup."

"Never heard of them," sniffed Jack.

"What!" said Wanda. "They're so famous."

"Really?" replied Jack. "Why's that? Do they save the world from danger every week like me?"

"No," said Wanda. "They solve crimes and catch crooks."

"So why can't they catch Ima Smartie instead of us?" asked Jack.

"Because they are down in Dartmoor on the trail of the Hound of the Basketballs," said Wanda. "Dartmoor is a scary place and it's haunted by a ghostly hound."

"Hey, that sounds fun," said Jack. "Maybe we should try catching ghosts instead of aliens."

Wanda shook her head. "We can't do that. We are the Alien Detective Agency," she said, "not the Ghost Detective Agency."

“Pity,” said Jack. Then he saw Sheerluck Holmes’ deerstalker hat hanging on a hook. He took it and put it on his head. “Hey, this hat is so cool.”

“Trust me. It so isn’t,” sighed Wanda.

Just then someone knocked on the front door.

Before Wanda could stop him, Jack opened it. An old woman stood on the doorstep.

She peered short-sightedly at Jack. “Are you Sheerluck Holmes?” she asked.

“No,” said Jack.

The woman pushed past him. “Then you must be Sheerluck Holmes,” she said to Wanda.

Wanda's mouth fell open. "Er, I'm ..." she began, but the old woman wasn't listening.

"You are probably wondering how I know who you are," she said. "Well, you don't have to be a detective to work out that if he's Dr Whatsup, then you must be Sheerluck Holmes! It's elementary, my dear!"

The old lady sat down in an armchair. "I'm Madam Grimm, the owner of Madam Grimm's waxworks museum. And there is something horrible in my Chamber of Horrors!"

## Chapter 3

# Too clever by half

"I thought the Chamber of Horrors in a waxworks was supposed to have horrible things in it," said Jack.

Madam Grimm nodded. "You are quite right, Dr Whatsup. And I do have werewolves, vampires, trolls, ghouls and goblins in my Chamber."

Jack swallowed nervously. "Gosh, they sound scary. I wouldn't want to spend the night down in the Chamber of Horrors with that lot!"

Wanda rolled her eyes. “Oh, get a grip, Jack. They aren’t real. They are made of wax.”

Madam Grimm nodded and smiled at Wanda. “Ah, that is why you are the famous detective and not him,” she said. “Tell me. How did you know my horrors are made of wax?”

Wanda took a deep breath and said through gritted teeth, “The clue’s in the name.”

“You’re clever,” said Madam Grimm. “I knew I was right to come to you.”

Jack decided it was time to show he was just as smart as Wanda. “So, if it isn’t the wax models of vampires and trolls that are causing trouble, it must be something else.” He raised one eyebrow at Madam Grimm. “Am I right?”

Madam Grimm gasped with amazement. “You are!”

Jack smirked. “I usually am,” he said.

Wanda sighed loudly. “Thank you, Dr Whatsup,” she said. “But the only way we are going to find out what’s really going on is to go to the Chamber of Horrors and look for ourselves.”

Chapter 4

# Horror in the chamber

The Chamber of Horrors in Madam Grimm's waxworks museum was a dark and spooky place. Vampires lurked in the shadows and a werewolf with blood-red eyes stared at Jack and Wanda.

"Good doggy," muttered Jack, patting its head. Then he tugged at Wanda's arm. "Hey, I'm sure that vampire over there moved."

"Oh, stop being a pain in the neck," snapped Wanda. "I'm trying to listen."

Jack froze. "What are you listening for?" he hissed.

"Well, not your silly chatter," she hissed back.

"It's not me chattering," said Jack. "It's my teeth. This place is really creepy."

Suddenly, a coffin lid creaked open and a creature from a nightmare's worst nightmare leapt out. It had purple skin, yellow eyes and sharp fangs. It glided towards them.

"I think Agent Darkstar was listening for me," it growled.

Jack yelped in terror and hid behind a model of a giant troll. His teeth were not just chattering, they were screaming HELP! at the tops of their voices.

Wanda didn't move. She folded her arms and stared at the evil-looking ghoul. "Hello, Ima," she said.

## Chapter 5

# The hat trick

The creature made a horrible gurgling sound, then began to melt. Wanda did a double-take. She ran over to the creature but it was now just a pool of melted wax. Wanda saw something in the wax. She knelt down and picked it up.

"I see you have found my dummy's radio-control microchip," said a strangely familiar voice.

Wanda spun round and saw Madam Grimm standing behind her. She had a hosepipe in her hand and she was pointing it at Wanda.

"You're not Madam Grimm – you're Ima Smartie," gasped Wanda.

"That's right," said Ima. "You two dummies walked into my trap and now I'll use this wax-spraying machine to turn you into wax models. You are going to be exhibits in the Chamber of Horrors – forever!"

She bent down and pressed the switch on the machine.

"I don't think so," yelled Jack. "I'm way too good-looking to end up in the Chamber of Horrors!"

He whipped the hat off his head and pushed it up the hosepipe's nozzle.

It made a brilliant plug. The machine began to shake and rattle.

"Quick, Wanda, get behind the troll," yelled Jack. "That machine is about to blow!"

They dived for cover just as the top shot off the sprayer. A fountain of wax shot up into the air and then splattered back down all over Ima!

“Hey, who’s the dummy now?” said Jack as he and Wanda stepped out from behind the huge troll.

Suddenly, a groaning noise came from an Egyptian mummy case in the corner of the Chamber.

“Oh no,” wailed Jack. “Please don’t let it be a mummy come back to life.”

“What’s up, Jack?” said Wanda. ”I thought you wanted to catch ghosts.”

But Jack didn’t answer. He was hiding behind the troll again.

Wanda shook her head and then strode over to the mummy case. She pulled it open and an old lady jumped into her arms.

It was the real Madam Grimm! Ima Smartie had locked her in the case when she took over the museum.

“I’ll crack the wax off Ima and then hand her over to the Galactic police,” said Wanda. She picked up the deerstalker. “Oh, and well done on the hat trick.”

“Get a grip, Wanda,” said Jack. “We were catching a crook, not playing football.” He shook his head. “How Ima thought you were the smart one I’ll never know! Maybe she’s not so much of a smartie after all.”

## Facts about Sherlock Holmes

Sherlock Holmes is the most famous detective in fiction.

Holmes is super-smart and logical.

His best friend is Dr Watson.

The Sherlock Holmes stories were written by Sir Arthur Conan Doyle.

Sir Arthur Conan Doyle was a doctor as well as a writer.

Sherlock Holmes lived at 221b Baker Street, in London.

Sherlock Holmes' biggest enemy was a villain called Professor Moriarty.

Sherlock Holmes called Moriarty the 'Napoleon of crime'.

Sherlock Holmes' deerstalker hat was the idea of the illustrator of the stories – not Sir Arthur Conan Doyle's.

The only villain ever to get the better of Sherlock Holmes was a woman called Irene Adler.

## Jack's joke

What is the name of the world's most famous dog detective?

Sherlock Bones!

## Questions

How does Jack like to relax?

Why doesn't anybody know what Ima Smartie really looks like?

What is Jack's favourite episode of 'Sci-Fi Spy Guy'?

What case are Sheerluck Holmes and Dr Whatsup working on?

What kind of hat does Jack say is 'cool'?

What does Jack want to catch instead of aliens?

How does Wanda know what the horrors in the Chamber of Horrors are made of?

How does Ima control the wax dummy?

How does Jack outwit Ima Smartie?

Who is in the Egyptian mummy case?